W9-ARY-250

THE STORYTELLER

BY JOAN WEISMAN

ILLUSTRATED BY DAVID P. BRADLEY

RIZZOLI
NEW YORK

Why was that lady watching them? Rama looked up from taking care of her four little brothers and sisters, who played on the pavement in front of the apartments. Almost the whole long day—every day—the old woman sat by her window, watching.

"Oh, Baby Maria, a cigarette butt!" Rama yelled. "I look away for one minute . . . Let me take that dirty thing out of your mouth!" Rama wiped her little sister's mouth. Meanwhile, the four-year-old twins, Diego and Cody, tussled and wrestled each other on the sidewalk. Cody scraped his knee, and they both began to wail.

Rama called to her other sister for help, but Reyes was at the corner of the block, jumping rope with the neighborhood kids, and didn't hear her. Reyes was almost eight, only two years younger than Rama. When they weren't jumping rope, Reyes and her friends played hopscotch or raced each other to the corner. Then, every couple of hours, they sat on the stoop and complained to Rama that they were bored.

Rama missed Cochiti Pueblo, where there were hundreds of things to do! After school she and her friends played hide-and-seek in the plaza, or they watched the women make pottery and bake bread in the outdoor ovens. Sometimes they acted out the stories that their grandparents told them at night—tales about Coyote the trickster, corn maidens, and the ancestors. "Grandfather," Rama whispered, "when Father is better we will come home again, and you'll tell us stories every night!"

"Rama!" Her mother called from the ground-floor window, interrupting her daydream. "I'll keep an eye on the little ones for a few minutes." She leaned out of the window and stretched out her arms so that Rama could lift Baby Maria up to her.

Rama was surprised her mother found time to watch the children in the middle of the day, in between washing clothes, cooking meals, and cleaning the apartment, and then working nights in the restaurant. Every afternoon she visited Rama's father in the hospital—they now lived in the city so they could be near him while he recovered.

"Rama, I brought a bowl of hot soup to Miss Lottie, the old woman on the third floor. She has been sick." Rama looked up and saw no one at the window. "Miss Lottie wants to talk to you, Rama. Go to her. I'll stay right here."

"Me?" Rama asked. "Why? Did we make too much noise?"

"Why don't you run up there and find out? Remember, I only have a few minutes."

Rama had never been to Miss Lottie's apartment. She stole up the stairs and knocked softly on the old woman's door.

There was no answer.

Rama wondered what she would do if Miss Lottie was very sick. What if she wasn't dressed? What if she was angry? Rama wanted to run for her mother, but she knocked again. Still no answer. Rama turned to run down the stairs. Then a voice stopped her, calling, "Come in, if you want to." Rama wasn't sure she wanted to, but she opened the door and stepped into the doorway.

Miss Lottie was sitting at the kitchen table, staring at a bowl of soup. Her hair was pulled into a loose bun; her blue eyes were watery. She was wrapped in a faded pink robe.

Rama didn't budge from the door.

"What did you want to talk to me about, Miss Lottie?"

"Why, Rama, I just wanted to talk."

Rama tried to think of something to say. She walked a few steps closer to the table. Miss Lottie stared at her with a steady but gentle gaze. Rama's grandfather used to watch her the same way. He would just look and look at her without saying a word, as if he had discovered a new plant on the mesa and he wanted to learn everything about it. Her grandfather wore his long gray hair in a bun. His eyes were bright and black, but something about Miss Lottie reminded Rama of him.

"I have an idea," Rama said, breaking the silence. "Wait a minute."

12

She rushed out of Miss Lottie's without bothering to shut the door and ran down the steps to her own apartment. Going into the bedroom that she shared with Diego, Cody, and Reyes, Rama sifted through her dresser drawer. She dug under blouses, sweaters, socks, three books, a pencil and tablet, and her blue plastic purse until she found something hard. It was about as big as her mother's shoe, wrapped in layers of white tissue paper.

PAINT·BY·NUMBER

Rama ran upstairs with the package and into Miss Lottie's kitchen. "I brought you something to keep you company," Rama said.

Miss Lottie carefully unwound the layers of tissue paper to find a pottery doll. It was an old Indian woman who sat with her legs straight out in front of her. Tiny dolls climbed on her arms and chest. Her mouth was wide open.

"Oh, how wonderful. How beautiful!" Miss Lottie exclaimed.

"It's a storyteller doll," Rama said. "In the pueblo we gather around our grandparents just like this. See how the sleepy little ones climb onto her lap?"

"How nice," said Miss Lottie. "How very nice to have all those snugly little children!"

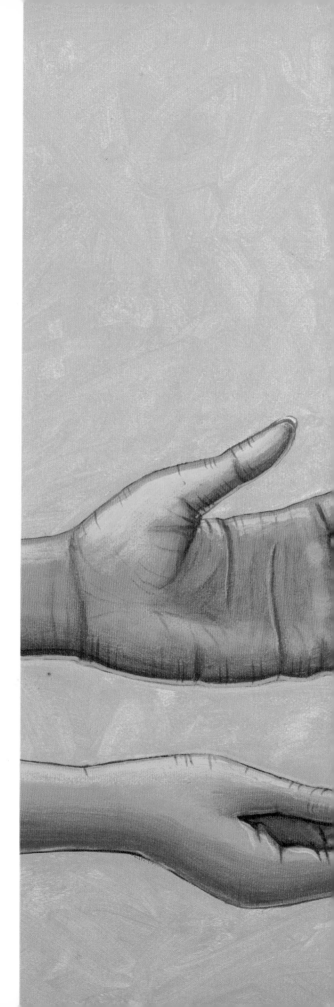

"My grandfather tells us stories about the old days, stories about how Spider-Woman led the first people from the under-ground world into this one through a hole in the earth called the *sipapu*. He says this is why our worship space, the *kiva*, has a hole in the center of its floor— to remind us of our journey.

"Some of my favorite stories he tells are about Kokopelli. He plays a flute and brings harmony to the people! Once, Grandfather showed me a picture of Kokopelli that the ancestors made on the rocks. . . ."

Miss Lottie listened to Rama's story. Then she said softly, "Rama, you can't give this away."

"I'd like you to keep it for me, Miss Lottie. The only safe place for it in our apartment is in my dresser drawer." Rama smiled. "If you keep my storyteller doll for me, I'll visit and tell you more of Grandfather's stories."

"That would be a great honor, Rama."

The next day Rama was outside with her sisters and brothers. When she saw Miss Lottie watching from her window, Rama waved to her new friend. And in that split second, Baby Maria grabbed an old candy wrapper from the sidewalk. Rama moaned. She picked up her sister, who howled and wriggled and squirmed to get down. Then Cody pushed Diego down on the sidewalk and sat on his chest. Diego began to cry. Before Rama could scold Cody, he burst out crying even louder than his brother. Just when Rama needed her, Reyes raced down the block with her friends.

Rama was ready to cry, too. Suddenly she looked up to find Miss Lottie standing on the stoop. The little ones hushed for a moment. They all stared at the old woman.

"You were so kind to me, Rama. Now I've come to see if I can help you."

The crying resumed and Rama wondered how *anyone* could help.

"Let me hold Baby Maria, Rama." Miss Lottie sat on the stoop and held out her arms. Baby Maria cried even louder when Rama handed her to Miss Lottie.

"The little mice are creeping, creeping." Miss Lottie said in a soft voice while her fingers crept along Baby Maria's fat arm. "The little mice are eating, eating, eating." And Miss Lottie pretended to eat with her fingers and feed Baby Maria. The crying stopped. "The little mice are sleeping, sleeping." Cody wiped his eyes and nose on his sleeve and climbed up on Miss Lottie's lap. Diego squeezed in next to Cody.

"The big gray cat came walking, walking." Miss Lottie's voice was scary and her fingers were moving slowly in the air. "The little mice go scampering, scampering, scampering." Her hands and fingers moved so wildly the three little children had to hold on tight.

By then Reyes was sitting at Miss Lottie's feet with four of her friends. "Again," they said. "Again!"

Miss Lottie played the finger game three more times, yet the children begged, "Again! Again!"

Rama sat down with them. "Miss Lottie, please tell us about long ago."

"Well, let's see. . . . One day, when I was about as big as Reyes here, I was walking the two miles home from our little one-room schoolhouse when a strong wind came up. It blew me clear across the road and into the ditch. I tried to stand, but that wind blew me right back down. So I crouched there trying to decide what to do, when. . . ."

The little ones snuggled in the old woman's lap and didn't make a sound. Wide-eyed, the older ones sat at Miss Lottie's feet and listened as she told them how she crawled on her hands and knees along the ditch for half a mile, to her Uncle Ezra's farm. "If Uncle Ezra hadn't been out gathering up the chickens in that ditch, who knows what would have happened."

"What did happen?" asked Reyes.

"Well, I don't remember how I got home. I suppose I stayed with Uncle Ezra and Aunt Belle until the wind calmed down, maybe overnight. Overnights were so much fun there. Uncle Ezra played his fiddle. Aunt Belle and I danced around the room until bedtime . . . ."

On every nice day after that the neighborhood children, Rama, her brothers, sisters, and Miss Lottie spent an hour on the stoop. Everyone took turns telling tales and listening carefully to one another. They shared stories about their favorite vacations, dreams, and memories. They talked about their friends and family, too. And sometimes they invented new stories just for fun.

At the end of summer Miss Lottie invited the children into her apartment to celebrate the recovery of Rama's father, and to say goodbye. Even though Rama and her family would return to Cochiti, the storyteller doll would stay in its place of honor—right in the middle of Miss Lottie's kitchen table.

"She sits where I can always see her," Miss Lottie said. "Thank you, Rama. Thank you very much."

"Now give me Baby Maria. Climb up here Cody, Diego. The rest of you—Rama, Reyes, you others—come close. Did I ever tell you about the time Benny the Bear Cub escaped when the circus came to town? Well, . . ."

Rama smiled because she knew the stories would continue.

THE PUEBLO STORYTELLER DOLL

Cochiti potters have made clay dolls and figurines since the late 1800s or early 1900s, but they were not known as "Storytellers" by the public. Today's Storytellers—the contemporary versions of those clay dolls—continue to represent and perpetuate the culture and traditions of the Cochiti people of New Mexico, but are now available to a wide audience.

My creation of the Grandmother and Grandfather Storytellers represents both the traditional and modern worlds in that many children do hang all over their grandparents, who tell them stories—the traditional way in which we pass on the oral history of our people. Beginning when the children are very young, storytelling takes place at night when the family is gathered next to a fireplace or at dinner time. Grandparents start a story by saying: "This happened long ago to the Cochiti people. . ." or "My great-grandparents experienced this. . . ." And soon they tell many stories, such as those about the trickster Coyote, Badger, the Spider-Woman, the giant man who ate children, and the traditional rabbit and deer hunts. This continues each night as the child grows, from one generation to the next, reinforcing the history and traditional life of the Pueblo people.

I enjoy making Storytellers because I feel closer to the Mother Earth—the strength of the spirits around me—since I am creating something from the earth. It also brings me great memories of my grandparents and the unselfishness of their time in teaching me the way of life of our people and how to respect the Creator's creations. By making the dolls I can bring harmony, happiness, and friendship to the many people and families who have my Storytellers in their homes.

Storyteller with 21 Babies by Ramus Suina

Ramus Suina
Director of Recruitment
Institute of American Indian Arts
Santa Fe, New Mexico

To the children in my life,
The old people in my life,
And those in between.
(You know who you are.)
—JW

For my wife, Arlene, with love.
And especially for my son, Diego,
Who has taught me the meaning of joy.
—DPB

RIZZOLI INTERNATIONAL PUBLICATIONS, INC.
300 Park Avenue South, New York, New York 10010

Library of Congress Cataloging-in-Publication Data

Weisman, Joan.
    The Storyteller / written by Joan Weisman; illustrated by
David P. Bradley.
        p.   cm.
    Summary: New to the city neighborhood, a Pueblo Indian girl
finds a friend in an elderly neighbor with whom she shares stories
of her people, and in return hears stories of Miss Lottie's life.
    ISBN: 0-8478-1742-3
    1. Pueblo Indians—Juvenile fiction.   [1. Pueblo Indians—Fiction.
2. Indians of North America—Southwest, New—Fiction.
3. Moving, Household—Fiction.   4. Storytelling—Fiction.   5. Old
age—Fiction.   6. City and town life—Fiction.   7. Neighborliness—
Fiction.]   I. Bradley, David P., 1954-   ill.   II. Title.
PZ7.W4464St   1993
[E]—dc20   93-20460
                                                         CIP
                                                          AC

DESIGNED BY BARBARA BALCH
EDITED BY KIMBERLY HARBOUR

Printed and bound in Italy